Say Hello to the Dinosaurs!

Ian Whybrow   Tim Warnes

Say Hello to the Dinosaurs!

MACMILLAN CHILDREN'S BOOKS

Are you ready with your roars?
Let's say hello to the dinosaurs!

Stegosaurus has plates on his back.
He swishes his tail as he stamps down the track.

Hello, Diplodocus!

Chomp, chomp, chomp!

Spinosaurus opens his jaws.
He waves his fan and his shiny claws.

Under the sea and close to the shore,
Swims a fishy Ichthyosaur.

Hello, Ichthyosaur!

Bubble, bubble!

Three pterodactyls glide in the sky.
Little ones hide when they fly by!

Triceratops is hard to beat,
With his three big horns and powerful feet!

Hello, Triceratops!

Stomp, Stomp, Stomp!

Here's the fiercest of them all.
Listen to my mummy's call!

Hello, Tyrannosaurus!

ROOAAARRR!

Now we'll play a little game.
I'll ask a question and you say the name!

Who's the longest dinosaur
in this book?

Which dinosaur has a fan
on his back?

Who's got a spiky tail that goes
swish, swash, swish?

For Milo Benwell-Froggatt – I.W.

For the mighty Levisaurus, and
long-lost Dinosaur Jack – T.W.

First published 2009 by Macmillan Children's Books
a division of Macmillan Publishers Limited
20 New Wharf Road, London N1 9RR
Basingstoke and Oxford
Associated companies throughout the world
www.panmacmillan.com

ISBN: 978-0-230-53138-3 (HB)
ISBN: 978-0-230-70739-9 (PB)

1 3 5 7 9 8 6 4 2

A CIP catalogue record for this book is available from the British Library.

Printed in China